Jo:Cj

From Your Work

auntie Rhonda

2020

How to Catch the Easter Bunny

Copyright © 2017 by Sourcebooks, Inc.
Cover design by Sourcebooks, Inc.
Written by Adam Wallace
Cover and internal illustrations © Andy Elkerton

Sourcebooks and the colophon are registered trademarks of Sourcebooks, Inc.

The art was first sketched, then painted digitally with brushes designed by the artist.

Published by Sourcebooks Jabberwocky, an imprint of Sourcebooks, Inc.
P.O. Box 4410, Naperville, Illinois 60567-4410
(630) 961-3900
Fax: (630) 961-2168
www.jabberwockykids.com

The Library of Congress Cataloging-in-Publication data is on file with the publisher.

Source of Production: Shenzhen Wing King Tong Paper Products Co. Ltd., Shenzhen, Guangdong Province, China
Date of Production: September 2019
Run Number: 5016206

Printed and bound in China.
WKT 10 9 8 7 6

How to Catch the Easter Bunny

From the *New York Times*
Bestselling Author and Illustrator

Adam Wallace & Andy Elkerton

sourcebooks
jabberwocky

I've been working long and hard
with all my peeps and crew.
We've made the eggs, and now I'm here
to bring them all to you!

My real name's a secret.

My friends call me E.B.

My special job means I must hide
my true identity!

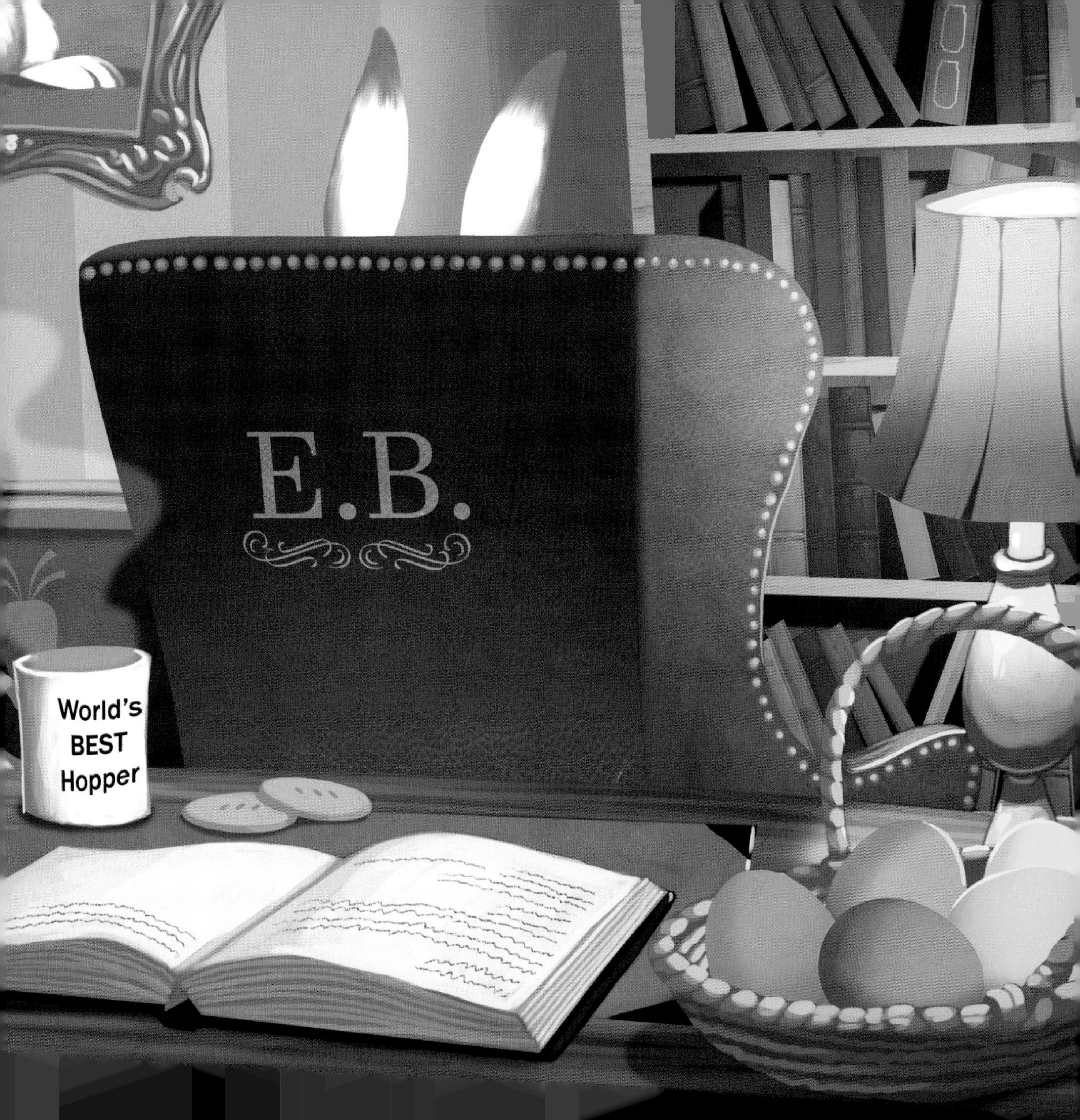
E.B.
World's
BEST
Hopper

Yes, I'm the **Easter Bunny**, and I'm coming to your home! If you have Easter spirit, then you just might see me roam!

This first trap is quite simple,
just carrots on a plate.
I'm *LIGHTNING FAST*! To catch me,
you'll need some better bait!

A hole that's covered by a rug
will never cause me strife.
Have you forgotten what I am?
Burrowing's my life!

Now this is much more like it,
a fully lit dance floor!
I'll do a little **hip-hop**,
then dash behind the door.

This next trap is quite clever,
made by brilliant engineers.
But it's hard to catch a bunny
who has SUPERSONIC ears!

You want to catch me for my eggs,
and magic basket too,
but I've been hiding Easter treats
since 1682!

This trap nearly gets me.
But check out all my hops!
Watch me dodge the flying fish
and **cherry yogurt pops!**

I switch my size, from two feet tall
to something small and gray.
Your Easter spirit is so strong,
you see me right away!

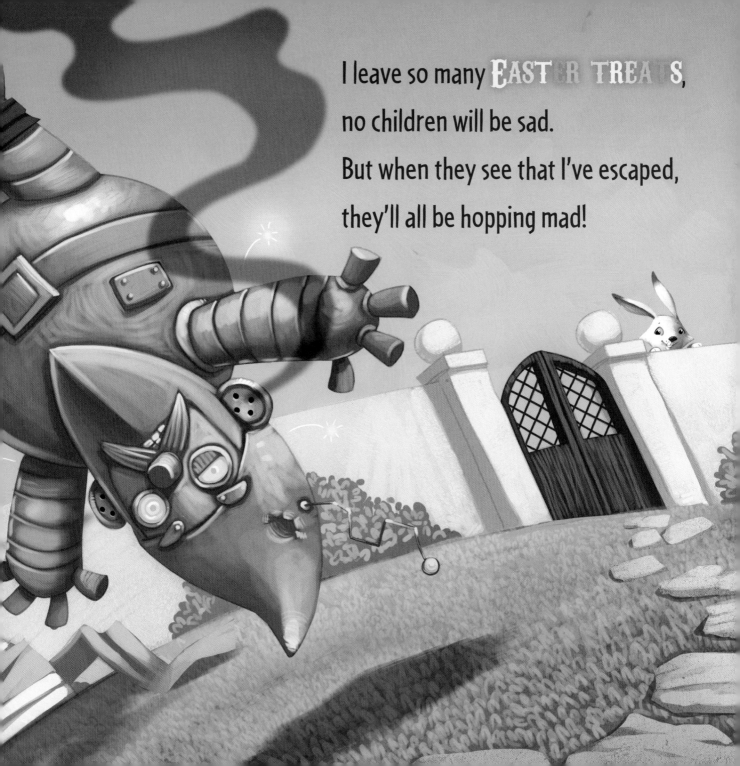

I leave so many EASTER TREATS,
no children will be sad.
But when they see that I've escaped,
they'll all be hopping mad!

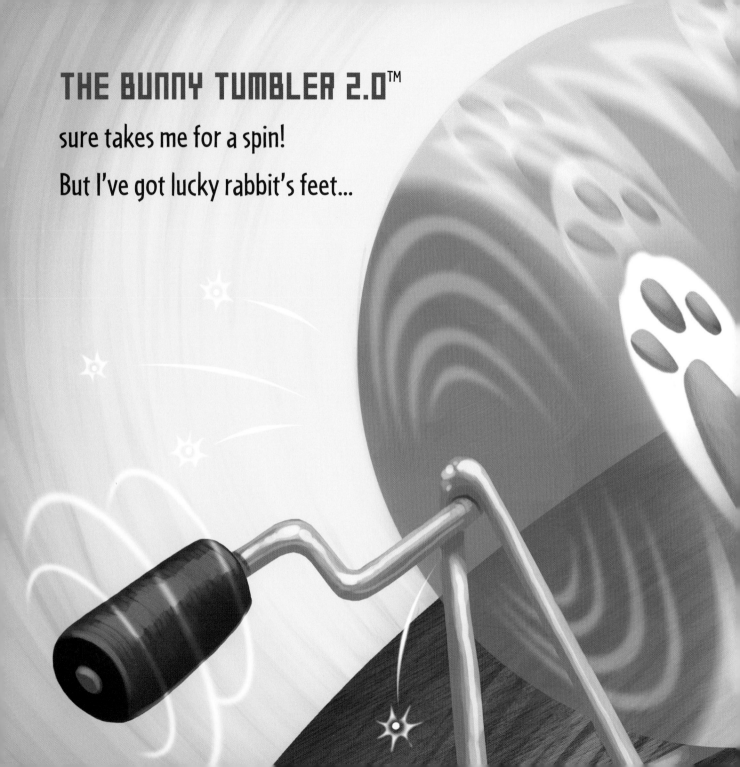

With all the treats delivered
to children big and small,
I've got one special stop to make
to my FAVORITE kid of all!

See you next year!